Sir Laughalot

Tony Mitton
Sarah Warburton

ORCHARD BOOKS

Sir Laughalot is a very brave knight.
He needs to find some foes to fight.

He has his **shield.**

He has his **sword.**

But Laughalot is feeling . . .

bored.

What can he do?

Where can he go?

Let's find Sir Laughalot a foe.

Here's a dragon, huge and green.
Its great big jaws look really mean.

Its muscly tail
could crush a house.

It makes a man seem
small as a mouse.

Sir Laughalot, you valiant knight, we've found a foe for you to fight!

ir Laughalot comes striding by.
He looks the dragon in the eye.

But then he starts to shake –

Oh dear!

Can Laughalot be full of fear?

Sir Laughalot seems
full of wriggles.
I think he's gone and
got the giggles.

He drops his sword,
and slaps his knee.

"Ha-ha!"
he laughs.
"Ho-ho!
Hee-hee!"

Sir Laughalot, this isn't right. You're meant to stand your ground and fight!

"But look," says Laughalot.
"Look there!

His nostrils have such silly hair.
It's sprouting out, so weird and wiggly.
It makes me go all weak and giggly."

The dragon starts
to see the joke.

His hairy nostrils
start to smoke.

That makes Sir Laughalot
guffaw,
and soon the pair are laughing more.

Sir Laughalot, this just won't do. We'll find another foe for you.

Here's a giant, big and tough.
His bristly face looks really rough.

His boots are big –

Kerrump!
Kerromp!

The trees all tremble when they stomp.

Sir Laughalot, you valiant knight, now, here's a foe for you to fight.

Sir Laughalot puts on a frown
to look the giant up and down.

He lifts his sword
to have a go . . .

but then he
d
r
o
p
s
it!

"Ho!
Ho!
Ho!"

Sir Laughalot, this cannot be. The giant's a frightful sight to see!

ut Laughalot says,
"Look at that!
He's wearing such a silly hat."

The giant hears what's just been said.
He pulls his hat right off his head.
The feather tickles at his nose
until he sneezes, snorts and blows.

That does it.
Giant and knight together
scream with laughter
at the feather.

Instead of battling to the death,
they grip their sides
and gasp for breath.

Sir Laughalot, we can't have that, such silly stuff about a hat.
We must be leaving. Off we go, to find a much more fitting foe.

*A*ha, a damsel in distress,
held captive by a sorceress.

Now, that's more like it, Laughalot,
for funny this is clearly not.

The sorceress is dressed in black.
A scary look she does not lack.

Her brows are knitted in a scowl
and on her shoulder squats an owl.

The damsel's in a tower up high.
We hear her sob. We hear her cry . . .

Hang on.

I know this may sound daft, but did she cry?

I think she laughed!

She thinks it's ever such a joke to see a metal-suited bloke.

Sir Laughalot is laughing too and waving to her,

"Hey! Yoo-hoo!"

The sorceress cries out, "Hooray! Please take this giggly girl away."

"Whatever happens, good or bad,
she laughs.
It drives me nearly mad.

Please take her off, and rescue me
from all her silly
'tee-hee-hee'.

Hey presto!
Here's a fine white horse
for you to take her on,
of course."

They mount the horse
      and off they trot,
the giggly girl
      and Laughalot.

And soon they're back
      at Laughers' Court,
where silly things
      are said and thought.

They laugh at that.
      They laugh at this.
The pair of them
      are both in bliss.

Says Laughalot,
      "My dear, who needs
those knightly fights
      and daring deeds?
Let's laugh a lot by night and day
and chuckle all our cares away."

So giggly girl and Laughalot get married soon. They tie the knot.

And soon they have two chuckly twins
who fill their lives with giggly grins.

So all ends happily ever after, with lots of love . . . and lots of laughter!

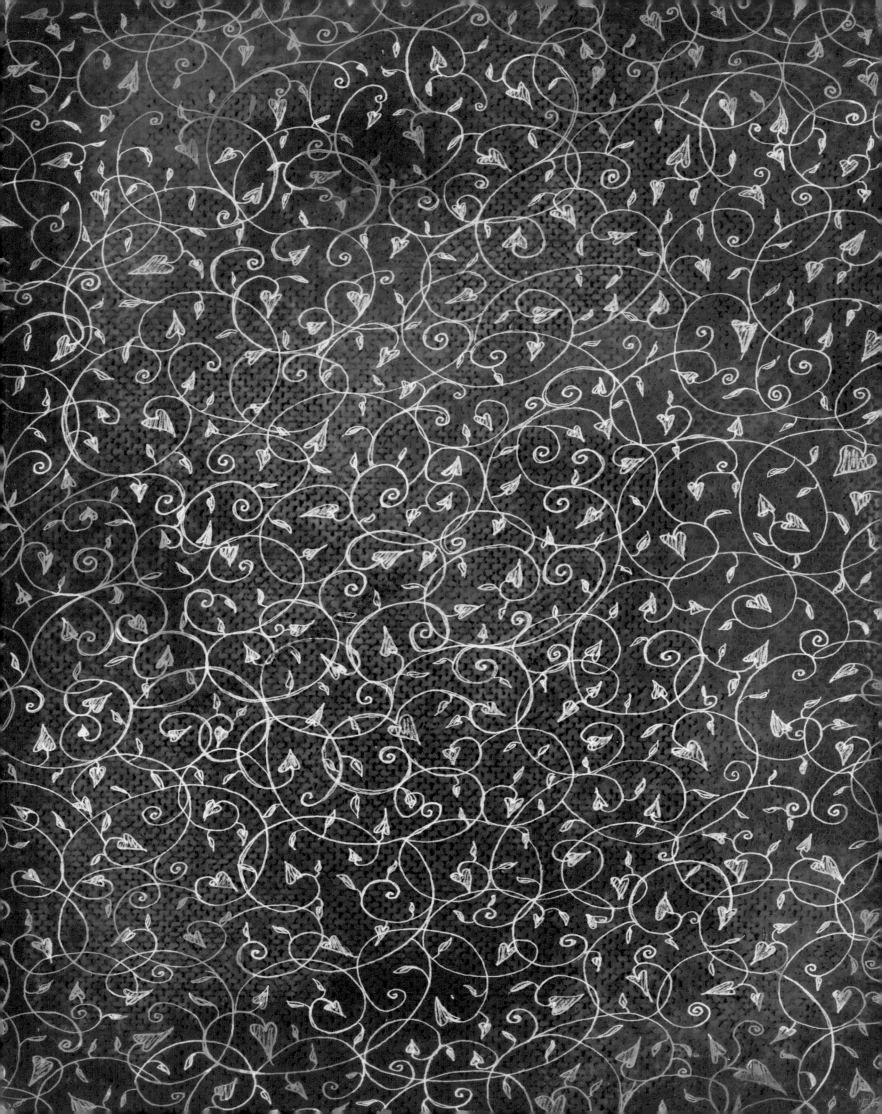